Pegleg Gets Stumped

Barnacle Barb & Her Pirate Crew

Written by Nadia Higgins
Illustrated by Jimmy Holder

magic Wagon

For Louis and his great ideas

visit us at www.abdopublishing.com

Published by Magic Wagon, a division of the ABDO Publishing Group, 8000 West 78th Street, Edina, Minnesota 55439.
Copyright © 2008 by Abdo Consulting Group, Inc. International copyrights reserved in all countries. All rights reserved.
No part of this book may be reproduced in any form without written permission from the publisher.
Looking Glass Library™ is a trademark and logo of Magic Wagon.

Printed in the United States.

Text by Nadia Higgins
Illustrations by Jimmy Holder
Edited by Bob Temple
Interior layout and design by Emily Love
Cover design by Emily Love

Library of Congress Cataloging-in-Publication Data
Higgins, Nadia.
  Pegleg gets stumped / Nadia Higgins ; illustrated by Jimmy Holder.
    p. cm. — (Barnacle Barb & her pirate crew)
  ISBN 978-1-60270-093-2
  [1. Pirates—Fiction. 2. Ghosts--Fiction.] I. Holder, Jimmy, ill. II. Title.
PZ7.H5349558Pe 2008
[E]—dc22
                          2007036983

Pegleg Pedro thrashed in his hammock. "Noooooo," the
sleeping pirate moaned. He swatted at the air. "Be gone!"
He plugged his nose. "Avast, ye smell!"

"Pegleg, wake up! Wake up!" Armpit Arnie shook Pegleg by
the stump.

"Wha . . . who . . . huh?" Pegleg opened his eyes. "Oooooh," he sighed in relief. "'Twas only a nightmare."

Armpit Arnie sniffed. "Pegleg," he said, "is that YOU?"

Pegleg Pedro sniffed too. "The smell—'tis real!" he screamed.

The pirates tried to figure out what the smell was. "'Tis not sweaty, not smoky, not salty, not fishy," Pegleg said. "In fact, 'tis kind of flowery, kind of—what's that word? Pretty?— I'm stumped!"

"Could it be?" Armpit said. "Could it be the ghost of the biggest pirate traitor to ever sail the seas?"

"Who? Who?" Pegleg asked. It felt like hermit crabs were crawling along his spine.

"Don't you know?" Armpit Arnie continued. His voice got soft and scratchy. "The ghost of Benestink Arrrnold. Arrrnold was a fierce, salty sea dog of a pirate. Then he started goin' strange. He picked flowers. One day, he even brushed his beard."

Pegleg Pedro gasped.

"Then he was gone. Legend has it he became one of the landlubbers, a seller of something they call 'perfume.'"

"Perfume? What's that?" Pegleg asked.

"No pirate knows. But on a foggy night such as this one, the ghost of Benestink Arrrnold is said to drift out to sea. And with him comes a smell to put fear in the nose of every pirate."

Pegleg and Armpit cautiously sniffed again.

"'Tis gone!" Pegleg said.

"And so the ghost of Benestink Arrrnold takes his leave," Armpit said.

The next night, Pegleg Pedro was relieved to see there was no fog in sight. "Benestink Arrrnold won't be hauntin' me tonight," he said.

"C'mon, Billy," he called to Barnacle Barb's parrot. "Time for your bedtime story."

Billy and Pegleg settled down to read *The Adventures of Furious George*.

Pegleg began, "This is George. He was a good little monkfish, because he was always furious."

Drip. Pegleg Pedro sleepily wiped his forehead.

"Did you feel that, Billy?"

Drip . . . drip . . . drip.

Pegleg looked outside. It wasn't raining. He checked the faucets. They were rusted shut as usual.

"I'm stumped!" Pegleg declared.

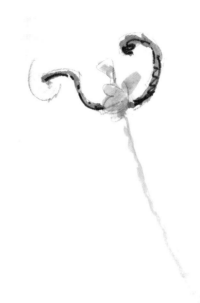

He crept over to Stinkin' Jim's hammock.
"Stinkin'! Stinkin'!" He woke the other pirate.
"Do you hear that?"

Stinkin' yawned. "You mean the *drip, drip, drip*?"
he asked, stretching.

"Aye," Pegleg Pedro said. "What is it?"

Stinkin' sat up. "'Tis the ghost of the unluckiest pirate
to ever sail the seas," he said.

"Who? Who?" Pegleg asked. Suddenly his hands felt like dead fish.

"That cursed pirate Hissy-Fit," Stinkin' Jim continued. "Hissy-Fit was known the seas over because he hated to swab the deck. When it was his turn, he whined and cried about it."

"Despicable!" Pegleg Pedro snorted.

"So one day, the Great Pirate of the Sea decided to teach Hissy-Fit a lesson. From then on, it was Hissy-Fit's turn to swab the deck every clear, moonlit night—like this one."

Stinkin' gave Pegleg a meaningful look.

"And? And?" Pegleg said.

"And here's the rub, me hearty—Hissy-Fit was not allowed to use any water. He was to swab the deck with his own tears," Stinkin' Jim continued.

"No!" Pegleg Pedro said.

"So each clear night—*drip . . . drip . . . drip*—he cried and he swabbed, cried and swabbed. But he never cried enough to finish the job. Then each morning, the sun would come out and dry Hissy-Fit's unfinished work."

"So he had to start all over again!" Pegleg said.

"Aye, if the moon be makin' the water sparkle like treasure," Stinkin' replied.

Pegleg Pedro and Stinkin' Jim sat quietly for a minute.

"The drippin's gone!" Pegleg said.

"And so Hissy-Fit be gone, too," Stinkin' said.

The next night, Pegleg examined the sky. The moon was peeking through a thin band of clouds. "Hmmmmm," he said. Nervously, he climbed into his hammock.

Pegleg closed his eyes and began to say his swears.

"Ye lily-livered landlubber," he practiced. "Ye groveling glob of guppy guts, ye twittering turtle turd," he chanted.

After a few minutes, he felt better. He opened his eyes. But what he saw made him feel like someone had dropped an anchor on his heart. A faint, flickering glow made shadows swim over the walls.

This time, Pegleg Pedro was too scared to look around for evidence. "I'm stumped!" he declared, pulling his blanket over his head.

Just then, Barnacle Barb came running by. She was waving a harpoon in the air.

"Did you see it? Did you see it?" she called out.

"See what?" Stinkin' Jim asked, rubbing his eyes.

"Me greatest enemy!" Barb declared.

"Who? Who?" Pegleg sat up.

"Noby Quick," Barb growled. "The Great White Snail. On nights like this, the hazy moonlight glows off her white, slimy body. It makes a light to chill even a pirate's heart."

Stinkin' Jim and Pegleg Pedro huddled together.

"One hundred years ago," Barnacle Barb went on, "I was just a wee pirate of eight. One night, the giant snail slithered aboard me ship. She covered everything in a great river of slime. When she slid away, she took with her me most-cherished toy."

"What was it?" Stinkin' asked.

"Me pretend fake leg," Barb said. "Since that day, I've been chasing the slippery thief over all the seven seas. But I've never been able to catch her."

The three pirates sighed. They looked around. "The light's gone!" Pegleg said.

"Aye, matie," Barb said, slinging her harpoon over her shoulder. "And so the hunt for Noby Quick continues another day."

The next night, Pegleg looked nervously up at the sky. It wasn't foggy, but clouds covered the moon. The pirate was so confused he didn't know what to do. He finally decided to go get a cup of warm milk.

But as Pegleg Pedro walked about the kitchen, his fake leg slipped on something. *Splat!* He found himself lying flat like a jellyfish on the floor.

The pirate sat up. Something like sea foam clung to the end of his stump. He looked across the deck. A line of foam led across it. It circled inside a tent made from old sails.

"Hmmm, 'tis odd I never noticed that before," Pegleg said. "'Tis right above me hammock."

Pegleg Pedro examined the foam some more. It was softer than sea foam. He sniffed it and gagged.

"Benestink Arrrnold?" he gasped. His heart banged like a hatch left open in a thunderstorm.

Pegleg followed the trail of foam. *Drip . . . drip . . . drip*. There was that sound! He inched closer to the tent. *Drip . . . splash . . . whoooosh*.

"Hissy-Fit?" he hissed. "But . . . but . . . ," He wondered about the *splash* and the *whoooosh*.

He crept up to the tent. It was glowing from within. Shadows swirled over its walls.

"Noby Quick?" he wondered. "But . . . but . . . how?" The moon was not in sight. The tent was not big enough to hold a giant snail.

Pegleg Pedro wondered what to do. Then he heard a familiar voice coming from inside the tent.

"Sail, sail, sail me ship
Across the seven seas . . . "

"Why, that sounds like Slimebeard!" Pegleg said. But Slimebeard was the grumpiest, most sour-faced pirate of the ship. "Could that be him singing?" Pegleg wondered.

Pegleg peered inside the tent. His jaw fell open like a whale about to catch a fish.

Was that his friend up to his beard in—bubbles? Pegleg Pedro slapped his forehead. So that was the pretty smell!

Was Slimebeard—playing in the water? So that made the *drip, drip, drip*!

And were those—candles all around? So that explained the eerie glow!

The mystery was solved. There were no ghosts. Noby Quick had not visited. Only one question remained: what do you do with a sweet-smelling pirate?

Sail, sail, Sail me ship
Across the Seven Seas
Yo ho ho, yo hee hee, yo ha ha Snort!
I'm jolly as can be!

Pirate Booty

- Pirates in the 1700s would often spend months at sea. As a result, they were a very smelly group of people! Bathing was not a regular part of their days. If they cleaned themselves at all, it was by taking a dip in the sea.

- Pirates really did have hooked hands, wooden legs, and eye patches—but so did a lot of other people. Medical treatments during the Golden Age of Pirates (1680–1725) weren't very good. Without antibiotics, there were few options for sick people. Amputation—cutting off the diseased body part—was often the only way to keep a person alive.

Pirate Translations

avast — stop
landlubber — someone who lives on land; not a pirate
monkfish — sea monkey
swab the deck — mop the deck
wee — small